04232-04

No ....................      Class ....................

Author ...............................................

Title ...............................................

# THE NIGHT OF THE UNICORN

*There it was: a sky full of shooting stars.*

# THE NIGHT OF THE UNICORN

## JENNY NIMMO

*illustrated by* TERRY MILNE

**WALKER BOOKS**
AND SUBSIDIARIES
LONDON • BOSTON • SYDNEY

First published 2003 by Walker Books Ltd, 87 Vauxhall Walk, London SE11 5HJ

2 4 6 8 10 9 7 5 3 1

Text © 2003 Jenny Nimmo   Illustrations © 2003 Terry Milne

The right of Jenny Nimmo and Terry Milne to be identified as
author and illustrator respectively of this work has been asserted by them
in accordance with the Copyright, Designs and Patents Act 1988

This book has been typeset in Minion Condensed, Goudy Hundred and Woodtype Ornaments 1

Printed and bound in Great Britain by Creative Print and Design (Wales), Ebbw Vale

British Library Cataloguing in Publication Data: a catalogue record
for this book is available from the British Library

ISBN 0-7445-9072-8

FOR MIMI, WITH LOVE - J.N.

## C H A P T E R   O N E

Amber woke up. It was very late. The house was quiet and so were the fields outside. And yet…

What had woken her? It wasn't a frightening thing. It was something special. She drew back the curtains and looked out of the window.

There it was: a sky full of shooting stars. They sped through the black night, winking and glistening, and although their voices were silent, Amber felt they were trying to tell her a secret.

She wanted to share the magic but couldn't bear to leave the window for one second. Besides, if she woke Kevin, her brother, he would only be grumpy. He was probably too old for magic stars, anyway.

It was as if the world had turned upside-down. The sky was bright and busy, while everything beneath it was hushed and still. No, not quite. Something moved.

Amber narrowed her eyes and stared. In the middle of the pale field there was a black blob, and the blob had moved. What was it? A rock? A branch? She couldn't make it out. Whatever it was, it had stopped moving now. Perhaps it was just an old dustbin-bag.

Amber watched the stars until the last one glittered and then vanished. Now and again she glanced at the blob, but it stayed where it was. As still as a stone. Amber got back into bed and fell asleep.

The blob was Amber's favourite hen. She was small and

black and her name was Hennie. When Amber had been very small, the dogs had seemed big and rough, and the cats had had mean claws and short tempers, but Hennie would let Amber pick her up and stroke her soft, dark feathers. She was the first creature Amber had ever loved.

Amber's mother had been very busy on the day of the shooting stars. When she had gone to collect the eggs, she had forgotten to close the chicken-house window. At first the ten chickens inside paid no attention to it. And then a smart, white hen called Clarrie began to grumble. The night air was cold, she clucked. The wind was sneaking through her feathers. She'd be so stiff she wouldn't be able to lay an egg for a week.

William, the cockerel, told her not to grumble. "Hold your tongue, chuck!" he said. "The night air hath a sweetness to it!"

William always talked like that. Hennie liked it, but the younger chickens complained that they didn't know what William was talking about. He was too old-fashioned, they said. Mind you, they never said this to his face. In the chicken-house, William was king. Until the night of the shooting stars.

When William told Clarrie to hold her tongue, she didn't. Instead, she said, "Hold your own tongue, loudmouth. I'm cold, and that's that!"

There was a shocked silence. You could have heard a feather drop. Hennie closed her eyes, hoping that Clarrie's remark would be overlooked and they could all go to sleep. But it was about to get worse.

"I'm cold too," said Anthea, a large red hen. "Call someone, William. Your voice is louder than ours."

"'Tis not the time for calling," William said gravely. "I know the laws."

"If you know so much, how come you can't get things done

around here?" said a voice. "For instance, why can't *you* shut windows?"

This time the silence in the chicken-house was tense and fearful, for the cheeky voice belonged to William's son, John, a speckled grey upstart. He was becoming rude and pushy with the hens, but until tonight he had never argued with his father.

"Be silent!" William ordered.

John wouldn't be silent. "You're past it, Dad," he muttered. "Every day you're getting older, and every day I'm getting stronger."

No more was said after this dreadful remark. The chickens tucked their heads under their wings and fell into an uneasy sleep. Sometime later, Hennie woke up to see William perched in the open window.

"William, what are you doing?" whispered Hennie.

"I'm going into the sky," he told her. "I have a fancy to fly high."

"But it's dark," said Hennie. "Will you come back?"

*"William, what are you doing?"* whispered Hennie.

"I think not," said William. He flapped his wings once, twice, and then he was gone.

Hennie was appalled. She jumped onto the narrow sill and peeped out. William had vanished. Had he really flown into the sky? Hennie looked up. She saw a shooting star. "A magic night," she murmured.

"Hennie, is that you?" Betty, a speckled hen, was just a year younger than Hennie. She was a wise and gentle chicken, and had always been a good friend to Hennie.

"William has gone," said Hennie. "I must find him."

"Not now," said Betty. "It's dark. Mort comes in the dark."

"William wasn't afraid of Mort," said Hennie. "Neither am I."

To tell the truth, neither she nor Betty knew who or what Mort was. No one had met him and lived to tell the tale. Usually Mort came at night, though he had been known to strike at dawn, or even at noon. It was said that he was red and that his gleaming eyes were the colour of gold. But who really knew? Mort was a mystery.

"Hennie, don't be foolish," pleaded Betty. "Mort should be feared. Mort is the end. If he takes you from us, I ... I don't know what I should do."

"Oh, Betty." Hennie hesitated. As she swung from foot to foot on the narrow sill, another star sped through the heavens. She thought of William with his tall, red comb and snow-white ruff. He wore a ruby-coloured waistcoat over his ivory shirt, and his long tail-feathers cascaded to the ground in gleaming stripes of green, black, purple and silver. Just lately, his amber-coloured eyes had been a little dull and he kept one of his smart yellow feet tucked beneath his feathers, as though it caused him pain.

"I must find him," said Hennie.

"You're too old," cried Betty. "Hennie, don't!"

But Hennie's black wings had lifted her from the window and now she was sailing through the air. It was a very enjoyable sensation, but it didn't last long. With a little thump she landed in the middle of the field.

For a moment, Hennie felt as though all her insides were in the wrong place. She took a few short breaths and looked up into the night sky. What a wondrous sight it was. Stars twinkled and glistened as far as the eye could see. What was there to fear on a night like this?

"William!" she called. "Are you there?"

William didn't answer. Instead, a chilling bark echoed from the trees beside the field. Hennie began to run. And then she froze. Instinct told her that running was foolish. To be invisible one must be still. As still and silent as a stone.

So Hennie stayed where she was: a small, black blob in an ocean of grass.

Far away, she could see Cherry Cottage, the house where Amber lived. In one of the windows a pale face looked out at the shooting stars. Could Hennie reach the house before Mort crept out of the trees?

Before she could make up her mind, the stars began to twinkle and flash so fiercely that Hennie thought they might explode.

And then they were calm, and a silence stole over the land – a silence so deep and mysterious it caught everything in its way. Trees, grass, wind, owls – all were hushed and utterly still.

A few moments later, when life had returned to the fields again, a furious barking could be heard on the wind. Hennie decided to make a break for it. She raced towards the house as fast as her small legs would carry her.

The barking came from seven dogs that lived three miles away, at Mr Grace's animal sanctuary. They slept in big comfortable baskets on Mr Grace's verandah, and all the twinkling going on in the sky had woken one of them up. He was a small, nervous dog called Peanut. He had a very troubled history, and anything unusual set him off. He yapped and whined until all the other dogs were awake too.

Perched on the verandah railings, seven wide-awake cats had been happily watching the fiery display. But Peanut's whining had ruined their fun and they began to scatter. Some took to their baskets, and others ran out across the grass. Then they stopped. For something extraordinary was beginning to happen. The noise of the dogs shivered and faded. The barking, yapping and howling became a gentle rustle, like the distant splash of waves on the shore.

The cats froze where they stood. Nothing stirred. And then the gate blew open and a cloud of stardust swept across the grass.

The dogs sat up. Their hair bristled and growls stuck uncomfortably in their throats. But the cats' eyes glowed like green fire when a dazzling white horse sailed over the gate. It made no sound at all when it landed.

The horse bowed its head and neighed softly.

*The horse bowed its head and neighed softly.*

The dogs and cats murmured their greetings. A breath of enchantment had settled on the garden and they were too afraid to speak out loud.

And then the creature bent to crop the grass and they saw the scar: a perfect circle beneath the snowy forelock, clearly signifying that this was something special. Not just a horse. But they would have known that even without the scar. The creature's bearing, its scent and its colour, the timing of its arrival on such an extraordinary night, all these things told them that this was a rare and wonderful animal.

"Do you have a name?" asked Peanut.

The other animals looked at him, surprised by his boldness.

"If I had one, I have forgotten it," replied the horse.

A large black dog called Groucho gave a discreet cough. "How – er – how did you lose your horn?"

"I haven't lost it. I'm so old that it has faded."

Did things fade when they got old? The dogs and cats glanced nervously at one another. Just to make sure they could still be seen.

"How old are you?" asked a tabby-cat.

"My years can be counted in hundreds."

This was too difficult to understand. The animals had no notion of what hundreds could mean. An uneasy mewing and whining broke out. A sheep and a donkey emerged from the orchard, and two brown rabbits stood up in their pen, their ears turned towards the commotion.

"I'm sorry," the horse said gently. "I'm afraid I've disturbed you."

"Oh, no. Quite the contrary," said Peanut, speaking for them all. "It's just that with all the twinkling and flashing that's been going on in the sky, it's been impossible to sleep."

"Hm. Would it help if I told you an old, old story – a tale of enchantment?" The horse's dark eyes glittered invitingly.

"Yes, yes!" they all cried. *"Yes, please!"*

And the sound of their barking and braying, their baaing and mewing travelled all the way across the fields to a small, black hen hiding behind a dustbin.

## CHAPTER TWO

Next morning, Amber told her family about the shooting stars.

"Why didn't you wake me up?" grumbled Kevin. "I wish I'd seen them."

"It was a special night," said Mr Vale, Amber's father. "They mentioned it on TV but I forgot all about it."

"You'll have to tell them at school," said Amber's mother. "I wonder if any of the others saw the stars?"

"I saw something else," said Amber.

"What?" asked Kevin.

"A black blob in the field. It was gone when I looked out this morning."

"A blob?" said Kevin. "It was probably a cowpat."

"We haven't got any cows," said Amber.

She was still trying to puzzle out what the blob could have been when she got to school.


Amber's teacher, Mrs Pritchett, said she had a special project for the children. They were to write about their pets. To illustrate their stories they must also make drawings or take photographs.

There was a buzz of excitement in the classroom.

"Hands up, those of you who have an animal of your own," said Mrs Pritchett.

This was a country school, surrounded by fields of cows and sheep; even those who didn't live on farms had cats or hamsters. All the hands went up – except Luke Benson's.

"Luke, don't you have *anything*?" asked Mrs Pritchett. "Not even a goldfish?"

Everyone turned to look at Luke. He shook his head. "No," he said.

"Perhaps you've got an auntie or an uncle with a pet? A dog or a cat? You could borrow theirs," suggested Mrs Pritchett.

"I haven't got any aunties or uncles," Luke said. He'd only been at the school for a few weeks, and he hadn't made friends with anyone yet. He was a tall, skinny boy with black curly hair and very dark eyes. Amber felt a bit sorry for him.

Mrs Pritchett was frowning. She told Luke to see her at break. "And now I want to sort out the kinds of animals you'll all be writing about," she said to the others. "We don't want twenty stories about cats, do we?" She smiled.

Amber wasn't often the first to put up her hand, but now she began to wave it frantically.

"All right, Amber, what have you chosen?" asked Mrs Pritchett.

"My black hen," said Amber in a rush. "She's twelve years old, so she's very special. I don't think she can lay eggs any more, but she's still very beautiful. She's got black feathers that sometimes look green and purple."

"Good. I can see you'll have a lot to write about, Amber." Mrs Pritchett went on to Charlotte, who was sitting beside Amber. Charlotte wanted to write about Cleo, her cat. Of course.

By the time Mrs Pritchett had got round the whole class it was time for break. Amber was afraid there were going to be arguments in the playground. Some of the children had been told to change the animals they'd wanted to write about. Charlotte was one of the unlucky ones.

"It's not fair." Charlotte slumped against the playground wall. "Just because I live on a farm, I've got to write about a sheep. What can I say about a sheep? I mean, I don't know sheep like I know Cleo."

"I suppose you're lucky to have any animal at all," said Amber, glad to have chosen something unusual. No one else had a hen.

"What d'you mean?" Charlotte glowered at Amber.

Luke Benson had just come out. His eyelids were red and he looked even sadder than he had in class. What had Mrs Pritchett said to him? What had *he* said to Mrs Pritchett?

"Luke hasn't got any animals at all," Amber murmured.

"That's not my fault," said Charlotte.

Several other girls had joined Amber and Charlotte. They all wanted to talk about their chosen animals, but Amber decided to change the subject. "Did you see the shooting stars last night?" she asked.

Nobody else had seen the stars. They all stared at Amber as if she had made it up.

"Of course we didn't see shooting stars," said Charlotte. "Did someone bang you on the head or something?" She was in a very bad mood.

"I saw them," said a voice.

Luke Benson was standing right behind Amber. He'd been listening to their conversation. "Brilliant, wasn't it?" he said.

Amber was so happy he'd seen the shooting stars too. She was beginning to think it had been a dream. "And they went on flying for ages, didn't they!" she said.

"Yeah." Luke began to talk about the names of stars, about planets and constellations; he knew a lot about the night sky. Amber wondered if he'd stayed up all night. Perhaps that was why he looked so weary.

Amber was so interested in what Luke was saying, she didn't notice the other children drift away from them, until, all at once, she realized that she was alone with Luke.

"I'm sorry you haven't got an animal," she said. "D'you want one of mine to write about? We've got a cat as well as the chickens."

"Mrs Pritchett says there are too many cats now," said Luke.

Amber was stumped. But only for a moment. "You could buy a hamster. I've seen one in the pet shop."

Luke shook his head so violently she thought it might fall off.

She had a flash of inspiration. "You could write about a bird. If you fed one on the window-sill, you could watch it, and…"

"I don't want a bird," Luke said vehemently.

"Oh."

Luke stared at Amber. She felt as though he were sizing her up. Maybe he wanted to tell her a secret and didn't know if he could trust her.

"What do you want, then?" she asked. "If you could have anything."

Luke went on staring, and then he said, "A unicorn."

A funny thing happened. The noise in the playground shivered and faded. The shouting and stamping, the screaming and singing became a gentle rustle, like the distant splash of waves on the shore.

"Why?" asked Amber, breaking the spell.

She couldn't be sure of Luke's reply because then the bell went, and he spoke very softly, but she thought he said, "Because they're magic."

"But unicorns don't exist," said Amber.

Luke just frowned and walked away from her.

The rest of the day went rather badly for Amber. For some reason Charlotte wouldn't speak to her, and Luke wouldn't even look in her direction. It was only the thought of her hen project that kept her going. She wished she hadn't said what she had about unicorns.

As soon as Amber got home she said, "I must go and see Hennie! I'm going to write about her."

"Oh." Her mother looked anxious. "Why does it have to be Hennie? Couldn't it be another chicken?"

"Of course not," said Amber. "Hennie's my favourite. She's the best and most beautiful."

"Oh dear," said Mrs Vale. "I'm sorry, Amber, but Hennie's gone."

"Gone?" Amber dropped her bag. "Where?"

"Well, we can only assume that…" Mrs Vale looked very unhappy. "Well, that a fox got her."

"Noooooooo!" shrieked Amber.

"William's gone too, and that would seem to indicate… Amber, I'm so sorry."

"She hasn't gone," cried Amber. "I won't believe it!"

As Amber tore out of the back door and down the steps, she failed to see a small black chicken beside the dustbin-bag. While Amber was running through the field, the chicken hopped up the steps and into Cherry Cottage.

*Amber failed to see a small black chicken beside the dustbin-bag.*

Where now? thought Hennie.

She saw a small door, slightly ajar, and popped through the gap. Now she was in a dark cupboard under the stairs. Hennie made room for herself between a brush and a mop, and settled down for a nice long nap. She'd been awake all night and was quite exhausted. Before she drifted off to sleep, she wondered if William was near by. Had he really flown into the sky, or had Mort…? Hennie refused to look on the gloomy side. William was alive, she knew it in her old hen bones.

## CHAPTER THREE

It was true. Hennie had gone. Amber counted the chickens. There were only eight, including John, the young cockerel. William had disappeared too.

The chickens crowded round Amber, begging for food. Amber usually carried an old crust or a piece of bread in her pocket, but today she had forgotten; she'd been so worried about Hennie.

"Where's Hennie?" she asked the chickens.

The chickens clucked hopefully.

"Did you see what happened?" begged Amber. "Oh, I wish you could talk to me. Where's Hennie? And where's William?"

The chickens turned away and scratched the earth, looking for grubs.

"It's useless talking to you lot," sighed Amber. As she walked back across the field she remembered the black blob she'd seen the night before. Could it have been Hennie?

When she reached the middle of the field, Amber began to search the grass. And there she found a shiny black feather. But what did it prove? She took the feather into the house and laid it on the kitchen table.

"Hennie's feather," she said, trying to hold back the tears, "but I couldn't find Hennie. Or William."

"I'm so sorry, Amber, darling," said Mrs Vale. "I'm afraid it was my fault. I forgot to shut the chicken-house window."

"How could you!" wailed Amber. "I'll never see Hennie

again! I wouldn't have minded if it was Clarrie or Anthea, or even John. But Hennie and William – it's a disaster!"

"Sit down and have your tea," said Mr Vale. "Hennie had a good innings. She was twelve years old."

"Innings?" growled Amber. "What innings?"

"Like cricket," Kevin explained. "It means she was around for a long time." Before Amber could start moaning again, he added, "I don't think a fox got Hennie. I mean, there was only one feather. When a fox strikes there are usually dozens of feathers, all over the place."

This was good news. There was hope after all. Amber sat down and swung her feet. They met something soft and squishy. Bart, the cat, rushed out from under the table, complaining bitterly.

"What's up with Bart?" said Kevin.

"I think I kicked him," said Amber, tucking into a sandwich. She felt so much better now. After tea she would write down all the things she remembered about Hennie – and tonight, perhaps,

Hennie would come back.

Still grumbling, Bart ran into the hall. He noticed that the door of the broom cupboard had been left slightly ajar. The Vales didn't like Bart to go into the cupboard. Twice he'd gone to sleep there and been shut in. And then he'd woken the whole family in the middle of the night with his yowling.

Bart, however, loved the broom cupboard. He always forgot his bad experiences and remembered only the dark, warm cosiness. The big cat crept into the cupboard and leapt for a space behind a pile of dusters.

"Hullo!" clucked Hennie.

Bart nearly jumped out of his skin. "What are you doing here?" he screeched.

"Keep your fur on," said Hennie. "And be quiet, *please*. I don't want *them* to know I'm here."

"Hens are supposed to be in the field," said Bart haughtily. "Clear out!"

"Don't be like that," said Hennie. "I'm looking for William. He disappeared last night. You haven't seen him, have you?"

"Course not. Now go back to the field, or I'll make a fuss."

"No." Hennie fluffed up her feathers and wriggled further into the nest of dusters.

"This is my place," said Bart.

"Well, I'm sharing it. There's plenty of room. You can sit on the mop."

"I don't *want* to!" Bart rushed back into the kitchen, wailing horribly.

"Shut up, Bart," said Kevin.

"He seems very angry about something," Amber remarked. "Look at his tail. It's waving about like a windscreen-wiper."

Kevin picked him up and carried him to the back door. Teeth bared and claws unleashed, the big cat wriggled and yowled. But he was no match for Kevin, who had an iron grip.

Bart was dumped on the back step, and the door was closed in his face. Not what he'd had in mind at all when he started complaining. Now he was locked out and the chicken was locked in. A very sorry state of affairs.

Hennie decided to move. She didn't like the thought of fat Bart jumping on her when she was fast asleep. She scrambled past the mops and brooms and out into the passage. There was a great deal of noise coming from the kitchen, and a very delicious smell. Obviously it was feeding time. Hennie walked towards the noise and the smell.

The kitchen door was open and Hennie stepped inside. For a moment she watched the Vales, who were all talking and eating at the same time. Nobody noticed Hennie. She thought of asking for food, but something told her that the family wouldn't be pleased to see her in the kitchen.

As luck would have it there was no need to beg. On the floor, just inside the door, there was a bowl of meat, conveniently chopped into small peck-size pieces. Hennie tucked in.

From the sill outside the kitchen window, Bart watched his dinner disappearing.

If Amber had looked down just then, instead of up, she would have seen Hennie. But Bart was making such a fuss that the Vales were all looking at the black cat, pacing outside the window.

"What's the matter with that cat?" said Mr Vale. "Why doesn't he go off and catch a few mice?"

Hennie scuttled out of the kitchen. She'd enjoyed her meal and now she really must find somewhere to sleep. Somewhere high, perhaps. At the end of the hall there was a staircase. Hennie

*From the sill outside the kitchen window, Bart watched his dinner disappearing.*

ran towards it. The steps were steep but not impossible. With a hop and a flutter she was on the first one. And then the next. Climbing stairs was easy once you got the hang of it, especially if you were equipped with wings.

## CHAPTER FOUR

Amber was not a tidy girl, which was just as well for Hennie.

The things at the bottom of Amber's wardrobe lay in a big muddle: backpack, jeans, shoes, books, toys – and Hennie. Amber didn't notice that her black woolly jumper had feathers.

She threw off her clothes (remembering, for once, to hang up her skirt), pulled on her pyjamas, brushed her teeth, washed her face and jumped into bed.

Just before she closed her eyes she thought she heard a little creak coming from the open wardrobe, but Amber was too tired to do anything about it.

"Probably a mouse," she said to herself. "I wish it was Hennie." She gave a big yawn and went to sleep.

When the house was quiet, Hennie clambered out of her hiding-place and continued her search for William.

Going downstairs was faster and easier than going up; Hennie fluttered into the hall in no time at all. Her first call was down the passage to the kitchen, where she hoped another meal would be waiting for her.

No such luck. Instead she found Bart glaring at her from a kitchen chair.

"Are you still here?" growled the big cat.

"I was feeling a bit peckish," said Hennie.

"Not half as peckish as I am," grumbled Bart. "You polished off half my supper and they wouldn't give me any more."

*Hennie found Bart glaring at her from a kitchen chair.*

"I'm truly sorry," said Hennie, who *was* truly sorry. "I don't normally go round stealing food. I'm usually well supplied with corn, but ever since I started looking for William my life has been all upside-down."

"So's mine," muttered Bart.

"If you could be a bit more helpful, I'd be out of your fur in no time," said Hennie.

Bart sat up. "What d'you mean, helpful?"

"I want to find William, that's all. As soon as I do we can go back to the chicken-house together."

"I have a lot of respect for William," Bart admitted. "If he's gone, it's for a good reason. Have you considered that?"

"No," Hennie confessed. "Although he did say he wanted to go into the sky. Many times. And last night there was all this magic in the sky: a-twinkling and a-flying. D'you think he's gone – up there – and can't get back?"

"I doubt it," said Bart. "Chickens can't fly *that* far."

"Then do you think…" Hennie paused. She could hardly bear to think of the other possibility, but she had to. "Do you think William has been…" Hennie swallowed. "Has been overcome by Mort?"

"Mort? What's Mort?" asked Bart.

"Mort is the end," Hennie whispered.

"The end?" Bart's fur stood on end. His fluffy tail went as rigid as a stick. "I see."

"Well, do you think it was Mort?" Hennie asked fearfully.

Cross as he was with the small black hen, Bart couldn't bring himself to add to her distress. She was a terrible nuisance, but she was also brave and loyal; she obviously deserved a bit of support.

"Nope," Bart said with conviction. "There's always a mess at 'the end', but that field's as clean as a whistle. I've been hunting there all evening, *seeing as I missed most of my supper.*"

"I'm sorry." Hennie's head drooped.

"Look here. If it'll help, I'll do a bit of scouting round

tomorrow," said Bart. "But right now I need my sleep, and, if it's all right with you, I'd prefer to do it on my own." He curled himself back into his chair and closed his eyes.

"Yes, it's all right with me," said Hennie wistfully. Cats were obviously more private than hens. She turned away from the kitchen and wandered to the end of the passage, where she found a soft black scarf that had fallen off one of the coat hooks.

Hennie scratched the scarf into a comfortable nest, tucked her head under her wing and went to sleep. She was still in her dark, cosy corner when Amber rushed out to the field the next morning.

"Hennie! Hennie, where are you?" called Amber. Once again she walked all round the field. This time she didn't even find a feather. Gloomily she walked back into the house and plonked herself down at the kitchen table.

"No sign of Hennie," she said. "I can't do my project without her."

"Why don't you choose another hen?" said Kevin. "Clarrie's quite pretty."

"Clarrie!" said Amber scornfully. "She's not a patch on Hennie. I can't do my work without her. I can't, I can't, I can't!"

"I'll help you look for Hennie after school," Kevin offered.

"Thanks," said Amber as gratefully as she could manage.

After breakfast, just as she was passing the kitchen door, Amber heard her mother say quietly, "You shouldn't encourage her, Kevin. I'm sure the fox has got Hennie!"

Amber clenched her fists.

When the children had gone, Bart walked up to Hennie and said, "In a minute the postman will arrive and we can make a start." He'd just had a large breakfast, so he was in a good mood.

Bart's timing was impeccable. The doorbell rang exactly one minute after he had spoken.

Mrs Vale went to open the door. The postman had a parcel and he handed her a slip of paper to sign. She was busy writing her name when a black cat walked out of the door, followed by a chicken. The postman was surprised. Chickens were not usually house pets. He didn't say anything to Mrs Vale, however, because he thought it was none of his business.

"Come on!" Bart called to Hennie.

Hennie hurried after Bart, who had now trotted out of sight round the corner of the house.

"There's obviously nothing to be gained by searching the

field again," said Bart. "We'd better try the other way. Down the lane and into the woods."

"Woods?" said Hennie. "Woods are dark."

"Yes," Bart agreed. "Good hunting territory."

"Hm," said Hennie.


At that moment Amber was marching gloomily through the school gates.

"What's up?" asked Charlotte.

"My hen's gone missing," said Amber.

"The fox has probably got her," said Charlotte.

"Don't *say* that!" Amber snapped.

"If you've got a photo of her, you could use that and just write about the things you remember about her," Charlotte said, trying to be helpful.

"I haven't got a photo, and I've *got* to find her," barked Amber.

"OK, OK!"

As they walked into class together, Charlotte said, "I've chosen a lamb for my project. I'm really getting to like him. I took his photo this morning."

"Lucky you!" said Amber.

At break Amber noticed Luke Benson wandering round the playground by himself. "I've got to ask Luke something," she told Charlotte.

"What?" asked Charlotte.

"It's kind of private," said Amber.

"Oh?" Charlotte looked cross and surprised at the same time.

Amber ran up to Luke. "Are you still thinking about a unicorn?" she asked.

Luke frowned at her. "What if I am?"

"I just wanted to say – don't give up." Amber glanced at Charlotte, who had turned her back and was talking to a group of girls under the chestnut tree.

"I wasn't going to give up," said Luke.

"Good. I've lost the hen I was going to write about, but I'm not going to give up either, and I was thinking, well … perhaps…" Amber swung from foot to foot, not quite knowing how to say what she wanted.

"Perhaps what?" Luke looked interested.

"If I help you to find a unicorn, perhaps you could help me find my hen."

"OK," said Luke, and for the first time ever, as far as Amber could remember, he smiled.

## CHAPTER FIVE

It wasn't long before Hennie realized she couldn't possibly keep up with Bart. His legs were much longer than hers, and he had bounce, something that seemed to be deserting her.

Halfway down the lane, Hennie's legs buckled and she sank to the ground. "Stop!" she clucked.

Bart looked back. Hennie was sitting right in the middle of the road. "You can't stay there," he said. "You'll be run over."

"I'm done in," said Hennie. "You're going too fast."

Bart sighed. "Move into the grass, then. I'll go on to the wood and scout around for a bit."

"D'you think William will be in the wood?"

"There's a good chance," said Bart, whose thoughts were really with chasing small rodents rather than looking for a cockerel.

Hennie heaved herself into the grass at the side of the road.

She'll be safe there, thought Bart. Having done his good deed for the day, he ran eagerly towards the wood.

Hennie waited. She dozed for a bit while the sun climbed higher and beat down on her glossy feathers. Then it began to get hot and Hennie moved into the shade of a tall hedge. She was very thirsty and wondered where she could find a drink. Soon she was hungry as well. She would have to walk on.

Keeping in the shadow of the hedge, Hennie shuffled through the grass. She couldn't see a wood. It must be much farther on, she thought. Or had Bart been lying to her? Almost before she knew it, the hedge and the grassy bank had ended and Hennie found herself bouncing down into the forecourt of a small petrol station.

Fixed to a lamppost at the entrance was a green litter bin and, beneath the bin, a scattering of crisps. Lunch!

Hennie ran to the feast and began to peck. She had eaten almost every crisp when she became aware that she was being watched.

Parked beside the door of the shop was an old Land Rover, and in the back, looking out at Hennie, were three dogs.

The dogs seemed quite friendly, so Hennie stepped closer to

the Land Rover, and looking up at the dogs she said, "I'm Hennie!"

"Gladys." "Groucho." "Peanut," barked the dogs.

"Have you seen a cockerel?" asked Hennie.

"Never!" "Nope!" "Several!" barked the dogs.

"Well, I'm searching for one called William," said Hennie, addressing the small white dog that had said it had seen several. "Will you look out for him?"

"Course!" "Yup!" "You're on!" said the dogs.

At that moment an old man came out of the shop carrying a large cardboard box.

"A chicken!" said the old man, surprised to see Hennie standing beside the Land Rover. "Sid, you never told me you kept chickens."

Sid came to the door and stared at Hennie. "Blow me," he said. "I don't know where that's come from, Mr Grace. Perhaps you'd better take it back to your sanctuary."

*Looking up at the dogs she said, "I'm Hennie!"*

Hennie decided she had better make herself scarce. She didn't want to be caught until she'd found William. As she ran away across the forecourt, she called, "William has a ruby waistcoat, a white ruff and a many-coloured tail."

"What *is* a cockerel exactly?" asked Groucho, when Hennie had gone.

"Haven't a clue," Peanut confessed.

"You shouldn't tell fibs, then," said Gladys, an elderly spaniel.

"We'd better come back and look for it," said Groucho. "I know the black thing was a chicken, so it might be one of those."

"The white horse will know," said Peanut.

## CHAPTER SIX

"Where were you?" Bart asked huffily.

He was waiting for Hennie when she came waddling back to the place where they had parted.

"I got hungry," she said, a little breathlessly. "I've had rather an exciting time."

Without waiting for Hennie to explain, Bart said, "I've spent half the day looking for William and the other half looking for you. As a result I haven't caught a single meal."

"I'm sorry," said Hennie. "I was talking to some dogs."

"Dogs!" Bart let out an angry wail. "What were you thinking of?"

"They were very nice, as a matter of fact," said Hennie. "They said they would look out for William."

"What?" Bart shook his head in disbelief. "I think you're having delusions, old girl. Either that or you've been asleep all morning. Dogs do not look out for chickens unless they want to eat them."

Because she needed Bart's help, Hennie meekly agreed that she had probably imagined what the dogs had said. But as she trotted along behind the cat, she found a little bounce had come back into her legs.

"Perhaps you should go back to the chicken-house," Bart suggested when they reached Cherry Cottage.

Hennie shuddered. "I can't go back there," she said. "Not

without William." She settled herself in a flower-bed.

"Well, you can't live in our house for ever," said Bart. "And it seems to me that … er…" He hesitated. Bart could be rather short-tempered but he had a good heart, and he didn't want to upset Hennie.

She knew what was going through his mind. "You were going to say that Mort has got William, weren't you."

"Yes," Bart admitted.

"Well, he hasn't," Hennie said with conviction. "Don't ask me how I know, but William disappeared on a night when magic was in the sky. Something very special happened, and whatever it was, it's protecting him."

"I see," said Bart, who hadn't a clue what Hennie was talking about. At that moment Amber and Kevin came through the gate.

"Hi, Bart!" called Amber. "Have you had a good day? I don't suppose you've seen Hennie, have you?"

Bart ran up to Amber and tried to tell her there was a chicken in the flower-bed, but Amber didn't understand.

"You've got a lot to say for yourself," said Kevin, tickling him under the chin. "What's going on, Bart?"

Amber picked him up and carried him into the house. "Here's Bart," she said, putting him on the kitchen floor. "He seems to be in a bit of a state."

"So am I," said Mrs Vale, pouring four cups of tea. "I think a bird must have got into the house. There are droppings everywhere, and I don't mean a sparrow or a blue-tit. This bird must be a big one."

"Really?" Amber was interested. "D'you think it was some-one's parrot, or a mynah bird?"

"I've no idea. But it made a mess in your wardrobe, on that lovely jumper you had for Christmas."

"That means it was in my bedroom?" cried Amber.

"It's not there now," called her mother as Amber rushed upstairs. "Come and have your tea."

Amber's mother had tidied all her clothes. There was no sign of a bird anywhere. But Mrs Vale had missed something. At the back of the wardrobe, in the darkest corner, Amber's fingers closed over something soft with a sharp tip. She drew it out into the light. It was a small black feather.

Amber flew downstairs. "It was Hennie," she cried. "Hennie was here!" She ran into the kitchen and held up the feather. "Look!"

Her family looked up from their tea and stared at the feather.

"It's certainly a black feather," said Kevin. "But what does that mean?"

"It means that Hennie's not dead. She's here, somewhere. In the house or the garden.

I'm going to look for her right now." As Amber raced into the garden, Hennie heaved herself up from the flower-bed and scrambled through the hedge. Bart was right. She couldn't live in the family house. She must find William, and then they would look for a nice place where they could live together in peace.

Hennie decided to try a different direction. William wasn't in the lane or the hedge, or at the petrol station. And Bart couldn't find him in the wood. He must have gone another way. Hennie crossed the lane and took a track leading through a field. At the end of the track there was a busy road. No place for a chicken. She ducked under a gate and found herself in a dusty-looking garden. There was no lawn to speak of, and no flowers. There were, however, many things to eat: woodlice, earwigs, a few worms, and – heavenly treat! – a rubbish-tip filled with bits of old bread.

Hennie stuffed herself and then nestled beside the rubbish-tip. A sad-looking house stood at the end of the garden. Hennie could not have said why it looked sad, except that it gave the impression of being unloved. The windows were dirty and the bricks hadn't been painted in ages.

Outside the shabby back door, a boy sat on a step, drawing. He had black hair and a serious face. Hennie watched him for a while, and then nodded off.

Luke looked up from his drawing-book. He was sure something had moved, over by the rubbish-tip. He hoped a cat would come strolling across the garden. He liked cats. His grandmother wouldn't let him keep one. "Too much trouble," she said. For her, everything was "too much trouble".

No cat appeared, so Luke went back to his drawing. He was using coloured pencils to fill in the background. In the foreground he had drawn a horse. Luke was good at drawing horses. He could remember every detail from the pictures he'd seen in books and magazines. And if he ever passed a field where a horse was grazing, he would watch and memorize every feature, even down to its hooves.

*Outside the shabby back door, a boy sat on a step, drawing.*

Luke had started doing this not long after his mother went away. She had told him she was going to marry someone with other children, but that she would come back for him when the time was right. That was a year ago. Luke had never known his father.

For a while Luke had been in care, and then he'd come here to his grandmother's house. At first his grandmother had been kind to him, but as the weeks passed it became clear to Luke that he wasn't wanted. He was a nuisance.

Luke told his grandmother to be patient. Soon his mother would send for him, he was sure of it.

And then his grandmother spoke the words that daily haunted him. "You've as much chance of seeing your mother as you have of riding a unicorn."

She'd laughed at her own bad joke, but seeing Luke's shocked expression, she had added, almost kindly, "So there it is. We'd better make the best of things."

That wasn't good enough for Luke. He decided to believe in the impossible. With precise and careful strokes, he now placed a horn on the horse's forehead: a long, delicate spiral that tapered to a point.

## CHAPTER SEVEN

It was getting dark. Hennie would soon have to find somewhere safe to roost. She didn't fancy sleeping on the fence, but there was a small tree growing beside the house. Hennie scrambled to the top of the rubbish-tip and hopped the short distance to the fence. Stepping carefully from post to post, she reached the end of the fence. From there it was an easy flight to the lowest branch of the tree.

Hennie nodded off. Tomorrow her journey would begin in

earnest. She would find William, even if she had to search the whole wide world.

She woke up just before dawn. A thin light was creeping over the distant hills, but the garden was still shadowy and mysterious. Something rustled close to Hennie's tree. She looked down and saw two small rabbits playing in the long grass. How charming, thought Hennie. She was about to close her eyes again when a strange feeling shot through her. Suddenly all her senses were ringing with fear. Her tawny eyes searched the garden. The rabbits were grazing now, oblivious to the approaching terror, and yet to Hennie the very air was charged with it. Cruel and murderous, it threatened to sweep her off her feet.

"Mort! Mort! Mort!" she cried.

The rabbits looked up. Now they, too, caught the scent of danger. They sat on their haunches, their eyes rolling in terror, unable to move.

"Run!" called Hennie. "Run, run, run, or it will be the end!"

Her voice cut through the little creatures' fear. All at once they leapt across the garden and through a hole in the fence.

The rabbits had gone, but the terror was still there. It was very close to Hennie. The scent of its hunger was overpowering. Something must die, and now there was only Hennie. She began to feel dizzy. If she looked into Mort's eyes she would be lost. And yet, terrified as she was, she longed to know if those eyes were really the colour of gold.

Luke found himself lying awake, trying to remember a dream. He was sure a chicken had come into it, but he had no idea why, and then he heard the frantic clucking outside his window. It wasn't a dream at all.

Luke jumped out of bed, turned on the light and flung open the window. Sitting in a branch, less than two metres away, was a small black chicken. Luke blinked in disbelief. What was a chicken doing here, right outside his window?

Amber had lost a hen. Could this be hers?

*The terror was still there... The scent of its hunger was overpowering.*

Luke put his hand out and made a soft clucking noise. "Come on, then! Come here, chicken!"

Suddenly his door opened and his grandmother looked in. "What are you doing?" she said irritably. "You woke me up. Get back to bed – it's only five o'clock!"

Luke quickly closed the window and drew the curtain. He didn't want his grandmother to see the chicken. There was no knowing what she would do with it. Kill it and cook it, if he knew her.

"I was hot," he said, "so I opened the window."

"What was all the noise?" she said. "Were you calling someone?"

"Calling?" asked Luke. "There's no one to call."

"Get back into bed." She turned away and closed the door with a sharp click.

Luke stood by the window until he heard a door close down the passage, then he quickly peeped through the curtains.

The chicken had gone.

After breakfast the next morning, Luke had a quick look round the garden. There was no sign of the black hen. Had he imagined it, then? He decided to tell Amber about it.

Luke caught up with Amber just as she was going into school with Charlotte. "Amber, I've got something to tell you," he said.

The two girls turned – Amber smiling, Charlotte frowning. Charlotte always made him feel like an insect.

"Hi!" said Amber.

"It's about your chicken," Luke said. "I think I might have seen her."

"Where? When?" Amber stepped closer as Charlotte walked off.

"You probably won't believe me, but…" Luke hesitated. He suddenly felt a bit silly. Who would believe he had seen a chicken in a tree?

"Go on," said Amber.

"Well, last night I heard this clucking, and when I opened my window and looked out, there was this little black chicken, sitting on a branch."

"Hennie!" cried Amber. "Can I come round to your house after school?"

"The hen's gone," said Luke. "I had to close the curtains when my gran came in – she doesn't like animals – and when I looked this morning, the tree was empty. So was the garden."

Amber didn't seem too disappointed. "Can I come anyway?" she said. "There may be a clue."

Luke wasn't sure. His grandmother didn't like unexpected visitors.

Amber was determined. "Please," she said. "Where d'you live?"

"It's the first house on the Belham Estate," Luke said reluctantly.

"Great! I'll get Mum to bring me round after school."

The bell went and they both rushed into class.

Charlotte gave Amber a funny look as she slid into the desk beside her. "You're not making friends with that boy, are you?" she asked.

"What if I am?" said Amber.

Charlotte scowled. "He's peculiar," she muttered.

"It's you who's peculiar," said Amber.

## CHAPTER EIGHT

As soon as she got home, Amber ran into the kitchen and announced, "There's a boy at school who saw Hennie in a tree outside his window."

"Could have been a crow," said Kevin.

Amber ignored him. "Mum, can you take me round to his house now?"

"Now?" Mrs Vale looked up from her pastry board. Her

hands were white with flour. "Can't it wait till after tea?"

"I told the boy I'd go round right after school," said Amber. "He might have caught Hennie already. He'll be waiting for us. His gran doesn't like animals, and if we don't go right now, she'll probably cook Hennie!"

Mrs Vale sighed. "We'd better be quick," she said, rinsing her hands. "Kevin, keep an eye on Bart. He's been trying to get into cupboards again."

"He's probably looking for Hennie," said Amber.

They climbed into the car and drove to the Belham Estate. Number 1 was a bit "ramshackle", as Mrs Vale put it.

"It's not Luke's fault," said Amber reproachfully.

They walked up a path overgrown with weeds and Mrs Vale rang the doorbell. The door was opened by a severe-looking woman, who said, "Yes?" rather irritably.

"I'm sorry to bother you," said Mrs Vale, "but my daughter says that your – er – Luke saw a chicken here?"

"The boy was probably lying," said the woman.

"No he wasn't!" said Amber fiercely.

"Amber's very fond of her hen," Mrs Vale explained. "Could she just take a look in your garden? Just to set her mind at rest. It wouldn't take long."

"There's no chicken here," the woman insisted. "But I suppose you can look." She led the way down a passage and opened a door at the back of the house.

Luke was poking about in the rubbish-tip. He looked rather gloomy, but when he saw Amber a broad smile lit up his face. "Hi!" he said. "I didn't think you'd come."

"Course I came," said Amber.

"I'll wait inside while you two search," said Mrs Vale. She turned to Luke's grandmother. "If that's all right?"

"Suit yourself," said the woman. She closed the door.

Amber surveyed the wild garden. "You've got a lot of weeds," she said.

"Not much else, is there?" Luke grinned. "Gran's too busy to do the garden."

They began their search close to the house and worked their way along the fence. As they peered through the clumps of nettles and brambles, Amber started to probe. She wanted to know why Luke lived with his grandmother, where he had lived before, why his mother had left.

No one had ever asked Luke so many questions. He tried to answer them, but he began to realize how little he really knew.

"Doesn't your mum ever write to you?" asked Amber.

"She sends me postcards," Luke said.

"Do you write back?"

"No," said Luke. "I don't know the address."

"Ask your grandmother," said Amber. "She's bound to know."

"She won't tell me."

"Make her. Maybe your mum doesn't know how you feel. Write to her and ask her to fetch you."

"I can't," said Luke.

"Yes, you can," said Amber.

She was very persuasive, this new friend. But Luke was afraid of the truth. If only he knew for sure that impossible things could happen. He turned away from Amber, shaking his head, and found himself staring at a small black feather. It was lodged in a bit of the fence. Luke carefully pulled it out and gave it to Amber.

"Hennie's feather," said Amber. "I'd know it anywhere. But where did she go next?" They looked over the fence. On the other side of a path, a field of maize stretched as far as they could see. There was no sign of any feathers.

"We'd never find her in there," said Amber.

They went back into the house, where Amber triumphantly held up the feather. Luke's grandmother grunted and said, "Beats me!"

Mrs Vale was eager to get home; there were cakes in the

*"Hennie's feather," said Amber. "I'd know it anywhere."*

oven and a cat on the prowl, and Kevin could be up to anything. "Thank you for letting Amber search," she said, and then suddenly, looking at the dark skinny boy in the doorway, she asked, "Can Luke have his tea with us?"

"Yes!" cried Amber.

Luke edged closer, smiling broadly.

"I'll bring him back in a couple of hours," said Mrs Vale. "If that's all right."

"I suppose so," said Luke's grandmother.

"Come on, Luke!" cried Amber, before the woman could change her mind.

Luke walked briskly through the door and followed Amber to the car. They settled themselves in the back while Mrs Vale got in and started the engine. Luke gazed out of the window, hardly able to believe his luck. He usually had to get his own tea, and he was a bit fed up with toast and cheese.

Amber began to point out places of interest: Charlotte's

farm, a haunted house, the road that led to the town where her father worked.

They had almost reached Cherry Cottage when they saw three strange dogs sniffing the grass beside a hedge.

"Did you see that, Mum?" asked Amber. "I've never seen three dogs out on their own before."

"They must belong to Mr Grace," said Mrs Vale.

"Who's Mr Grace?" asked Amber.

"He saves abandoned animals," said Mrs Vale. "When no one wants them any more, Mr Grace takes them in and looks after them. I'd better give him a call when we get back. He'll be wondering where they've got to. Whatever are they doing all the way out here?"

"I think they're looking for something," said Luke.

"Everyone seems to be looking for something these days," said Amber. "Ever since the night of the shooting stars."

The sky had turned very black, and tiny drops of rain began to splash against the windscreen.

## CHAPTER NINE

Groucho, Peanut and Gladys dragged themselves through the front gate of the sanctuary. The rain had finally made them turn back. Now their coats were sodden.

They padded round the side of the house, where they were was greeted by a chorus of "There they are!" "Where were you?" "Himself was so worried!" "Look at you, now, you're dripping!"

The other four dogs and the seven cats were sheltering from

the rain on the verandah. One of the dogs, a poodle, kept yapping, "Why? Where? Where've you been?"

The commotion brought Mr Grace out of the house. "There you are," he said, when he saw the three truants. "What *have* you been up to? Someone saw you right down by the petrol station."

Peanut and Groucho ran up the steps, tails wagging, but as Gladys didn't seem inclined to move any further, Mr Grace had to push from behind while she clambered up the four steps and out of the rain. Then he fetched a towel and began to rub Gladys's long hair.

"You're chumps, that's what you are," said the old man. "All three of you. What were you thinking of?"

When Mr Grace went indoors to cook the animals' supper (they always had home-cooked meals), one of the cats said, "While you three were away, the horse told us another tale of enchantment."

"Oh?" Peanut tried not to show his disappointment. "What was this one about?"

"The past," wheezed George, an overweight Labrador.

"About a king called Arthur," said a one-eared cat. "It was wonderful."

"I'm sure it was," sighed Peanut. The horse's tales of enchant- ment never failed to cast a spell. Sometimes it spoke of a time when magic monsters roamed the earth and elves and goblins lived in the woods. It told these stories as if it had really seen these things. And yet how was that possible? wondered Peanut.

Mr Grace brought fifteen bowls of shepherd's pie onto the verandah. It took three journeys, and he had to hurry because the last animals were becoming rather anxious. The fifteenth bowl was for Mr Grace himself. He always ate with the cats and dogs, just to keep an eye on them. George was particularly greedy and would often try to steal another animal's food. Then a fight would break out, and although the cats and dogs had learned to live with one another, when the dogs got cross some of the cats would run away, leaving their suppers. Mr Grace sat on the top step and looked down at the orchard.

The donkey, the sheep and the rabbits had already been fed, but the white horse ate only grass. It had turned its head politely from the carrots and sugar lumps that Mr Grace had offered.

"Where have you come from?" the old man murmured. He had asked everyone in the village if they knew of a white horse with a scar on its forehead. They were all as mystified as he was.

When supper was over, Mr Grace gathered up the bowls and took them indoors to wash. It had stopped raining and the sky was clear and still. The sun dipped behind the maize fields, leaving clouds of gleaming scarlet spread across the horizon.

The animals found it unsettling. They smelt danger. Their hair began to bristle, their noses twitched uncontrollably and a low growling and mewing broke out.

The white horse trotted out of the orchard and looked over the gate. It tossed its head, snorting anxiously, and, like an echo, a strange cry came out of the fields.

"Cock-a-doodle-doo! Cock-a-doodle-doo!"

"A cockerel in trouble," said the horse.

"Cock-a-doodle-doo! Help! Save me!" cried William.

"A cockerel is only a bird," said a ginger cat. "What does it matter?"

"*Everything* matters," said the horse sternly.

Under the horse's gaze, the cat felt ashamed. It hung its head and slunk into a corner.

"Dogs, bark!" commanded the horse.

"Bark?" They looked at each other in confusion. What reason was there to bark?

*The white horse trotted out of the orchard and looked over the gate.*

"Bark as loud as you can," ordered the horse. "Howl as if your life depended on it. Now!"

How could they refuse? The seven dogs threw back their heads and the longest, loudest, most awesome howl rose out of their throats and filled the air.

An eerie silence followed. Cats and dogs stood shoulder to shoulder, holding their breath and watching the fields.

Another cry came rippling towards them, closer this time. "Cock-a-doodle! Help! It's Mort. It's Mort!"

"FLY!" bellowed the horse. "Use your wings, cockerel! Fly!"

This time the dogs needed no prompting. They howled again. Straining their throats, they let loose a series of howls that would have done credit to a pack of wolves.

Two things happened. Mr Grace came rushing out of the house, and something flew over the hedge and flopped onto the ground at the horse's feet.

A bedraggled, tail-less cockerel looked up and breathed,

"Friends, I owe you my life," and then the poor creature collapsed in a heap.

"Good grief!" Mr Grace came running over to the tattered bird. "A cockerel? Where did that come from?" He picked it up and gently carried it indoors.

"Is it dead?" Peanut asked the horse.

"No, not dead," said the horse. "Your voices saved it. You frightened death away."

The dogs were silent. It was not in their nature to save birds, and yet they felt rather proud of themselves.

"Did you shut the chickens' window, Mum?" Amber asked her mother. "And the door?"

"I did. I won't forget again, I promise."

They were driving back to Belham, and there was a strange glow in the sky; a sinister gleam that was both beautiful and dangerous.

"It's going to rain again," said Mrs Vale. "There's going to be a whopper of a thunderstorm tonight."

Luke was very quiet. He hadn't had such a good time in ages. Bart, the cat, had jumped on his lap every time he sat down. Even Amber's brother, Kevin, had been nice to him.

Amber said, "D'you want to come round at the weekend, Luke?"

Luke nodded. "Shall we look for your hen?"

"Yes, and your unicorn."

"OK." He smiled. "We'll go on searching until we find them."

"Yes. And you can come round every weekend until your mother fetches you. Can't he, Mum?"

"If he wants to," said Mrs Vale.

"I do," said Luke. His mother was never going to fetch him –

*unless the impossible happened.* But at least he wouldn't be a nuisance to his grandmother at weekends.

As they sped past the entrance to Charlotte's farm, they failed to notice a small black hen sitting beside the gate.

## CHAPTER TEN

Hennie was so tired she could barely move. She had come a very long way. Last night she had looked into the eyes of Mort and lived – but only just. He had been so close. Another second and she would have tumbled out of her tree and landed at his feet. But a boy had opened a window and saved her.

When the boy spoke, Mort slunk away. Hennie could sense his dark shape gliding round the side of the house. The boy shut the window and Hennie flew onto a shed in the next-door garden. She felt safer, but not safe enough to sleep. As soon as it was light she fluttered down into a field.

Hennie's third journey was long and lonely; the wheat in the field stood tall and dense, and Hennie had little idea of where she was going. Eventually she found one of her own feathers on a narrow track between the fields. Must be nearly home, thought Hennie. She would have continued up the track, but a family of badgers came trotting towards her and Hennie was so shocked that she dashed into the fields again. For the rest of that day, Hennie battled through a forest of tall, spiky plants. Occasionally she stopped for a feast of earwigs or caterpillars, but she could feel the wind sharpening and the sky beginning to glower above her. She knew rain was on its way and dared not rest for long.

At last Hennie found herself beside a road. A blue car passed her; it looked familiar. When the car had gone, Hennie ran across the road towards an open gate. Was this the gate to Amber's house? No. Hennie sank into the grass, too tired to walk another step.

The little hen slept for a while, but when she woke up she knew she must find a safer place. The blue car passed her again, this time going the other way. Was that Amber looking out?

"What are you doing here?" said a voice.

Hennie nearly jumped out of her feathers. Charlotte's white cat, Cleo, was glaring down at her.

"I'm lost," said Hennie. "I thought this was my home."

"Well, it isn't. It's mine," said Cleo. "Now push off!"

"Couldn't I stay here?" asked Hennie. "Just for the night."

"Out of the question," sniffed the white cat. "Move on, you scruffy old thing." Before Hennie could reply, she was surprised to see the cat back away, mewing anxiously. Hennie was beginning to wonder what she could possibly have done to frighten her, when something bounded past her and swiped the white cat on the nose. "Yowl!" cried Cleo.

"Don't ever speak to our hen like that again," screeched Bart.

"*Your* hen?" hissed Cleo. "Since when have you taken to keeping chickens?"

"I've always kept them!" said Bart.

He leapt at Cleo again, and this time she wasn't taking any chances. Bart was bigger and stronger than she was. Off she ran, screeching, "I've had enough of chickens. There's been a dirty old cockerel in our barn for two nights, and now this!"

Hennie pricked up her ears. Had she heard right? A cockerel

in the barn? Could it be William? While the two cats fought it out in the yard, Hennie fluffed up her feathers and, with a great effort, pulled herself to her feet. The barn stood at the end of the yard. Hennie headed towards it.

She had almost reached the barn when there was a clap of thunder, and a torrent of rain came hurtling out of the clouds. Hennie gathered her strength and ran to it. The door was shut fast.

Battered by rain and quaking at the thunder, Hennie dragged herself round the side of the barn. Here a pile of sacks gave her a little protection from the weather. She heard a girl's voice calling, "Cleo! Cleo!" The voice was drowned by another clap of thunder.

Hennie crouched between the sacks and waited for the storm to die. It was a long, long night. The thunder rolled away but the rain kept coming. In spite of her shelter, Hennie's feathers were soaked through. At first light she listened for William's voice, but no sound came from the barn. William had gone. With a burst of energy, Hennie sprinted across the yard and squeezed through a gap in the hedge. She didn't want to have another argument with the white cat.

She found herself in a field of dripping maize. The ground was wet and soggy, but Hennie soon found a path leading through the field. Other animals had taken this route. Quite a few of them. All day Hennie trudged along the path, sometimes stopping for a meal, sometimes dozing. Towards evening, just as

she was thinking of a good long sleep, she saw something gleaming ahead of her. A pile of long, coloured tail-feathers lay scattered across the path. They looked like William's.

"Oh, William!" Hennie sank to the ground. Her

head drooped. "Mort," she murmured. When that dreadful name was uttered, it seemed to bring an air of menace rustling through the field. Mort was close. Hennie could feel danger in every feather. Veering off the path, she dashed into the forest of maize. But which way to go? She curved left, then right. Panic sent her running in circles.

Closer! Closer! The scent of Mort was overwhelming.

Terror almost swept Hennie off her feet; it drove her, screeching, towards a tall green hedge, a hedge too high and too thick for Hennie.

"Help!" she cried. "Help! Mort!"

From behind the hedge a familiar voice called, "Sweet, my chuck, spread thy wings and fly."

"William?" Hennie could hardly believe it. "Oh, William, I've found you."

"Fly!" called William.

Hennie couldn't fly. Hennie couldn't even move. She was old

and tired and had walked too far. Mort's stealthy and terrifying approach had paralysed her. Faintly, she called, "Goodbye, dear William."

From their sanctuary behind the hedge the animals murmured in consternation. All of them felt the deadly presence beyond the gate.

William, his pride restored – if not his feathers – stood crowing from the steps of the verandah. "Save my wife! Oh, prithee, save my wife!"

The dogs and cats looked at the white horse.

"What shall we do?" asked Gladys. "Shall we bark?"

"It's too late for that." The horse tossed its head and then reared up, beating the air with its hooves.

The other animals backed away. All at once, the gentle horse looked different. Immensely powerful and proud.

"Follow!" it commanded, and it rushed at the gate, which fell apart with a crack as though struck by lightning.

The dogs and cats, and even the donkey, bounded over the broken gate and into the field.

A great tide of barking swept round Hennie, and though her eyes were closed she could sense that Mort was going.

Through the wind that blew across the maize field, the voices of dogs and cats – yes, even cats – made a fierce sort of music. On and on it went, round and round the field, and Hennie knew that Mort was being chased away. But she was still afraid; she still kept her head down and her eyes closed. A pack of dogs could be just as dangerous as Mort.

*Through the wind that blew across the maize field*

*he voices of dogs and cats made a fierce sort of music.*

And then everything went very still. A deep silence descended on the field, and Hennie thought, Perhaps this is the end?

But it wasn't the end. Hennie opened one eye. She saw something tall and white: a horse. It had a long, noble face and a strange mark on its forehead.

"Don't be afraid," said the horse.

Hennie found that she wasn't afraid. In fact, she felt much better. She stood up and shook out her feathers. And now she could see that a great many cats and dogs were peering at her from behind the horse.

"Thank you!" she said. "You chased Mort away."

The dogs and cats murmured "You're welcome!", "A pleasure!" and other comforting words.

The white horse nodded at a gate lying in the grass. "Go into the sanctuary, Hennie!"

Hennie stepped lightly over the broken gate.

And there was William!

## CHAPTER ELEVEN

On Saturday morning Mrs Vale told Amber she had some news. "Charlotte's mother says they've had a strange cockerel roosting in their barn," she said.

"I bet it was William," said Amber. "What happened to it?"

"The cat chased it away, apparently."

"That Cleo is worse than a dog," muttered Amber. "They didn't see a hen, I suppose?"

"No, but they found some black feathers!"

"Hennie!" cried Amber. "Can I go and look? We've only got two days to finish the animal project now."

Mrs Vale agreed to take Amber round to Charlotte's farm, but first they had to collect Luke.

Luke was sitting on his front step when Amber and her mother arrived. He'd been waiting there for half an hour, eager to get out of the house, where his grandmother was in another bad mood.

As soon as Luke was in the car, Amber said, "Did you ask for your mother's address?"

"Yes. Gran said she wasn't sure where it was, but she'd look for it."

"You've taken the first step," said Amber cheerfully. "Now all you have to do is write the letter."

"I suppose," said Luke, without enthusiasm. He was surprised when they turned off the road and drove into a farmyard.

"Where are we?" he asked.

"It's Charlotte's house," Amber told him. "They saw a cockerel in their barn, and some black feathers. So we're going to start looking from here."

"Oh." Luke wasn't sure about this. Charlotte had never been very friendly.

Mrs Vale parked beside a large blue tractor and the two children followed her into the farmhouse. Amber's camera swung from a cord round her neck. She had come prepared.

In the kitchen, Charlotte's mother poured two glasses of orange juice and two cups of coffee. Mrs Vale was an old friend, and soon the two mothers were chatting happily about school trips, salad dressing and the weather.

Charlotte appeared, carrying a white cat. She frowned at Luke. "What's *he* doing here?" she asked Amber.

"He's going to help me look for Hennie," Amber said. "D'you want to come?"

"No," said Charlotte. "I've got to groom Cleo. Look what your horrible Bart did to her." She pointed to a scratch on the white cat's nose.

Amber ignored this. "Well, can you show us where you saw the cockerel, then?"

Charlotte sighed and stroked Cleo's nose. The cat flinched.

"Go on, Charlotte," said her mother. "Show them the barn and where we saw the black feathers."

Charlotte sighed again. "Come on, then," she said.

The white cat put its paws on her shoulder and stared back at Luke and Amber as they followed Charlotte across the yard. She led them round the side of an old barn and pointed to a row of plastic sacks. "The feathers are over there," she said, "and this is the barn where the cockerel was."

Amber knelt and looked between two sacks. And sure enough, there was a neat pile of black feathers on the ground. Amber took a photo. "I expect she had a bit of a scratch there," she said, straightening up. "Where did the cockerel go?"

"Cleo chased it into the field," said Charlotte. "The gate was open."

Amber ran up to the gate and looked out at the field of maize. The two chickens could be anywhere. And then she saw a single black feather, lying on the path through the field.

"Another feather!" cried Amber, taking a quick photo. "Come on, Luke!"

Charlotte watched disapprovingly as Luke and Amber climbed over the gate. "You *can* open it, you know," she said.

"We didn't *want* to open it," said Amber. She started to run.

Luke raced after her, but in a few minutes they both slowed down and began to look for more clues. They noticed that some of the maize had been broken and flattened, as though trampled by a great many creatures. Soon after this, they came upon a spray of long shiny tail-feathers.

"Oh!" cried Amber. "It looks as if the fox has got William."

"Maybe the fox only got feathers," said Luke. "Maybe the cockerel got away."

"That's true," said Amber gratefully. She took a photo of the feathers.

At that moment a familiar sound floated eerily across the field. "Cock-a-doodle-doo!"

The call was repeated, this time accompanied by a whole chorus of sounds: braying, barking, howling and clucking.

"Whatever is it?" Amber stared at Luke.

"Come on," said Luke.

They set off again, this time with Luke leading. The path took them through the field and past a small wood. Gradually the sounds died down and by the time they had reached a wild-looking hedge, only an occasional bark could be heard.

Set in the hedge was a small gate – recently mended, by the look of it. Amber peered over it. At the end of a long garden stood a

house with a verandah, and there, dozing in the sun, were a great many dogs and cats. There was also a very old man, sitting on a step. A tabby-cat slept on his lap.

At the other end of the garden, a sheep and a donkey were grazing in an orchard; and sitting under an apple tree were William and Hennie. Amber lifted the latch on the gate and walked into the garden. Luke followed her. Some of the dogs barked at their entry, but the old man hushed them.

Amber rushed over to Hennie and scooped her into her arms. "Hennie," she murmured. "I've found you."

Hennie gave a weary but cheerful cluck and tucked her head into her feathers.

The old man stood up, putting the cat on the step behind him. "Hullo, there," he said. "And who might you be?"

"I'm Amber," said Amber, "and this is Luke, and this is Hennie, and that" – she pointed at William – "that's William. They're my chickens."

"Wondered where they came from," said the old man. "Pleased to meet you, Amber and Luke. I'm Jim Grace." He shook their hands.

"Mum told me you look after animals that no one wants," said Amber. "But I do want Hennie and William. Can I take them home now? You see, I'm doing this project at school on Hennie."

The old man scratched his head. "Do you like biscuits?" he said at last.

*"Hennie,"* Amber murmured. *"I've found you."*

"Yes," said Luke and Amber.

"Follow me."

Baffled, the two children followed the old man to the steps, where he motioned them to sit. He went indoors and brought out a plate of home-made biscuits. Luke and Amber took one each and the old man settled himself between them.

"It's like this," he said. "If a creature runs away from home, there's something wrong. Oh, I'm not saying it's your fault," he assured Amber, who was looking rather offended. "Maybe something happened in the chicken-house – an argument or a fight. Maybe there's a new cockerel around."

"John," said Amber. "He's a bit pushy."

"That's it, then." He nodded at Hennie. "Those two are old."

"Very old," Amber agreed. She stroked the soft black feathers. "She must have walked so far. All the way from our house to Luke's, and then Charlotte's, and then here. How did she do it?"

"There's more to animals than we'll ever know," said Mr Grace. "William and Hennie are never going to be happy with a young chap pushing them around, are they? William's not well, in my opinion. His comb's sagging, he's lame in one foot, he doesn't see too well and he's lost his spurs, had you noticed that?"

"No." Amber felt ashamed.

Mr Grace patted her hand. "There, don't you worry. I've got an idea. I've made this comfy roost for them in a shed. How about you let your old Hennie and your old William stay here with us. And you can come round and see them any time you want. How about that?"

Amber thought long and hard. She began to like the idea. "Yes," she said. "That would be good."

Luke suddenly stood up. He stepped down onto the grass and took a few paces into the garden. As Amber watched him, she began to get a strange tingle down her spine. The air became very still and a vast silence swept over the sanctuary.

A white horse had emerged from the orchard. It began to approach Luke. The other animals watched intently. Not a whisker moved, not a sound escaped them.

The horse came right up to Luke and bent its head, and Luke just stood there, too amazed and enchanted to speak. Slowly he brought up one hand and stroked the soft, white nose. "It's a unicorn," he breathed. "Look!"

Amber saw the perfect circle on the creature's forehead: a small patch where sparse, dark hair had grown over an old scar.

"It's lost its horn," she said.

"So I noticed," said Mr Grace. "It arrived when the sky was all a-twinkle with flying stars."

"Oh," said Amber thoughtfully. "A lot happened that night."

Luke said, "Could I … would it let me ride it?"

"Don't see why not. It's a very gentle creature." Mr Grace came down the steps and cupped his hands to make a stirrup. "Up you go, then."

Luke put one foot into the old man's hands and swung the other over the white back. For a moment he sat there, lost for words, his shining eyes gazing into space. And then he leant forward and touched the circle of dark hair. "I'm riding a unicorn," he murmured.

"Yes," said Amber. She put Hennie down on the grass and took a photo of Luke.

The unicorn carried Luke twice round the garden, and then he slid off its back. Luke's smile was so wide, Amber thought his

*"I'm riding a unicorn," Luke murmured.*

face would crack. "I've got to take a photo of you and Hennie," he told Amber.

One by one, every animal in the sanctuary was photographed. Amber and Luke took it in turns, but Amber took the last photo of all: Mr Grace surrounded by his family. It was time to go home. Amber had almost forgotten her mother, waiting in the farmhouse and probably drinking too much coffee.

The children said goodbye to Mr Grace and began to walk home through the fields. Before they had gone far, something made Luke stop and look back. The unicorn was standing at the gate. It seemed to be watching them.

"Look," said Luke. "The unicorn."

When Amber turned, the white creature tossed its head and gave a gentle neigh.

"It *is* a unicorn, isn't it?" breathed Luke.

"Definitely," said Amber. "I'll give you the photo of you on its back. Your project will be the best."

"No, yours will be," said Luke.

"It doesn't really matter whose is the best, does it?" said Amber.

"No."

They walked on in silence for a while. There was so much to think about, so much to do. And then Luke said, "I'm going to write a letter when I get home."

They began to run.

## CHAPTER TWELVE

It was one of those nights when the moon turns everything silver.

William and Hennie sat side by side in their new house. It was smaller than the one at Cherry Cottage, but very comfortable.

"I came a long way to find you," Hennie told William. "I wanted to take you home."

"Sweet chuck," sighed William. "This, now, is home."

"A good home," Hennie added.

*They watched the unicorn step across the grass.*

From a small window beside their perch, they could see the garden and all the dogs and cats asleep on the verandah.

The unicorn was cropping the grass near by. When it saw that William and Hennie were awake, it gave a soft whinny and trotted up to them.

"I have to leave now," the unicorn said.

"So soon?" said Hennie.

"I have a long way to go."

"We'll miss you," said William.

"You are brave creatures. It's been a privilege to know you."

William bowed his head. "Fare thee well," he said.

They watched the unicorn step across the grass. It turned, briefly, to look back at them and they saw, on its forehead, a glittering, delicate horn.

The moon bathed the unicorn in dazzling light, and it soared above the gate so smoothly, it might have had wings.

JENNY NIMMO lived on a chicken farm until she was six, when she was sent away to school. On leaving school she became a drama student, and later joined the BBC as a photographic researcher. She also worked as an assistant floor-manager and a director of children's programmes. A chance meeting with the Welsh artist David Wynn Millward led to marriage, three children, a converted watermill in Wales – and chickens.

Jenny has kept chickens for twenty years now. She finds them quirky and emotional, and compares their passionate henhouse dramas to Shakespearian tragedies. The story of Hennie and William was inspired by one such drama.

TERRY MILNE was born in Cape Town and studied illustration at Stellenbosch University. Her numerous books for children include Jenny Nimmo's *Dog Star* and the picture book *The Toymaker*, written by Martin Waddell. Terry recently moved to Oxford, where she lives with her architect husband and their two young daughters, Ella and Anya.